# Animal Legends

Retold by
## Carol Watson

Adapted by Gill Harvey

## Illustrated by
## Nick Price

Reading Consultant: Alison Kelly
University of Surrey Roehampton

# Contents

Chapter 1:            3
The cat and the rat

Chapter 2:            18
Why monkeys live
in trees

Chapter 3:            36
The rabbits and the
crocodile

# Chapter 1

# The cat and the rat

You might not believe it now, when cats chase rats and rats hate cats, but long ago, they were best friends.

One cat
and rat lived
very happily
together on
an island.
The island
had all they
needed. There were birds for
the cat to chase...

...and plenty of
juicy plants for
the rat to
nibble with
her sharp
front teeth.

There was only one problem.
There wasn't much else to do.
Most days they were bored.

Then, one morning, the rat
had an idea.

Why don't we
look for somewhere
else to live?

Purrr-fect! But how
would we get there?

The rat thought about it.
How could they leave the
island? Then she twitched her
whiskers and smiled.

"That's easy," she said.

We'll make
a boat from
the trunk of
a tree!

The rat
gnawed at
a tree until
it toppled
over...

Timber!

...and the cat scratched out

the inside
of the
trunk, so
they had
somewhere
to sit.

Finally, the rat nibbled two branches and made them into oars. They were ready to go to sea.

The cat stepped into the boat and took the oars. Then the rat pushed the boat out onto the waves.

"Here goes!" said the cat.

Be careful!
I don't want to
get wet.

"There's nothing to worry about!" said the rat. "We'll be fine."

They rowed and rowed until
it grew dark.
The cat was
so tired, he
fell asleep.

Oh no!
We forgot to
bring food.

But the rat felt hungry. She
was so
hungry, she
began to
nibble the
side of the
boat.

But she made such a noise,
she woke up the cat.

"Don't worry!" squeaked the
rat. "You're dreaming."
So the cat went back to sleep.

The rat was very greedy and kept on gnawing at the boat. Munch... munch... munch...

Suddenly, she stopped.

The rat had eaten so much, she'd made a hole in the boat.

Water started to slosh up through the hole and the boat began to sink.

The cat woke up with a start. "I'm wet!" he squealed.

We're sinking!

We'll have to swim!

They had to leap from the
boat and
swim for
their lives.

This is all your fault, rat!

The cat was very angry. He
hated getting wet. "I'm going
to eat *you*
when we get
to shore!" he
spluttered.

Help!

The rat scrambled up the
shore and ran to a sandhill.
She dug a hole as fast as she
could and dived into it.

The hole was too small for
the cat to squeeze into. "I'm
safe!" thought the rat.

But the cat didn't give up so easily. He peered into the hole. "I'll wait for you, rat!" he called. "You'll have to come out sometime."

I can wait all week!

So, he sat and he waited... and waited...

16

...and waited. But the rat never came out.

She dug a tunnel all the way through the hill and ran out on the other side.

Whew! I've escaped.

And that is why, today, a cat will sit for hour upon hour, waiting to pounce on a rat.

## Chapter 2

# Why monkeys live in trees

Many years ago, the king of the jungle was a gorilla named Naresh. All the animals wanted to marry his daughter, but she didn't know who to choose.

One day, Naresh spotted a big wooden barrel sitting on the grass. "That's new!" he said and looked inside.

Oooh! What's that?

The barrel was full of greasy water. Naresh took a sip. It tasted of fire. "Fire water?" he said. "That might be useful."

Naresh took the barrel home
and called the other animals
together.

"I have a
barrel of fire
water!" he
said. "And it
will help us
decide who's
to marry my
daughter."

Whoever
can drink the whole
barrel may have my
beautiful daughter
as his bride.

The animals were very excited. Everyone wanted to try. They pushed and shoved closer to the barrel, but the elephant got there first.

"Just watch. This will be easy!" he boasted.

The elephant dipped his
trunk into the barrel. He
sucked up some fire water
and... sneezed.

Ah-chooooo!

"Oww!" he snorted, spraying
water everywhere. "It stings!
No one could drink that!" And
he rushed off.

The hippopotamus tried next. "I live in the river and drink water all the time," he said. "I'm not scared of a bit of fire water!"

So he took a big mouthful...

Urrrgghhh!

...and almost choked. He spat out the fire water and ran to the river to cool his mouth.

Next, the warthog stepped forward.

"I can eat or drink anything," he bragged.

No problem!

He drank from the barrel and coughed. "Ugh! That's horrible!" he shouted.

Yeeeuk!

"What fools you are," cried a voice. It was the leopard. "And you're all far too ugly to marry the king's daughter."

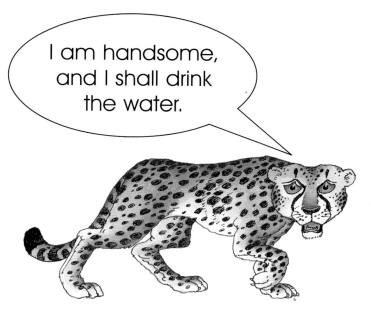

I am handsome, and I shall drink the water.

He stepped up to the barrel and just as quickly stepped back again. Even the smell of fire water made him feel sick.

The other animals laughed
at the leopard and he crept
away in shame. Then a little
voice piped up.

It was a tiny monkey. The
animals stared at him. How
could he drink the water?

Naresh smiled. "You can try if you want," he said. "But you must drink all the water and finish it today."

I don't want a single drop left.

"May I drink a little at a time with rests in between?" asked the monkey.

Naresh was a fair king. "Of course," he said.

So the tiny monkey climbed
onto the barrel. The other
animals gathered around,
grinning. This was going to
be funny.

But the monkey seemed very
sure of himself.

The monkey gulped a large mouthful of the fire water, then ran off into the bushes.

"Where's he going?" the other animals wondered.

After a few moments, the
monkey was back. He climbed

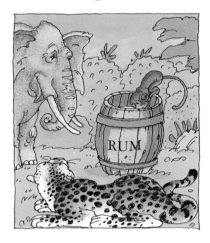

up the side
of the barrel,
took another
gulp of fire
water...

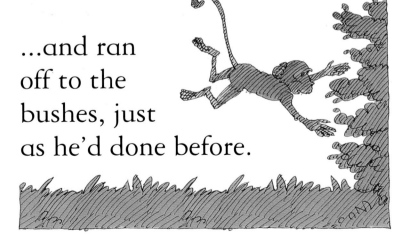

...and ran
off to the
bushes, just
as he'd done before.

But Telinga, the monkey,
had a secret. He wasn't alone.
Behind the bushes sat a whole
tribe of monkeys, who all
looked exactly the same.

Each monkey took turns
to drink some of the burning
fire water.

By the end of the day, the barrel was empty. The other animals were astonished.

"Now I shall meet my bride," said Telinga proudly.

The monkey stood before the old gorilla. "Well done," said Naresh. "You have completed the task. You may marry my daughter."

But his daughter didn't look too pleased.

I've got to marry *him*?

Ah, my lovely bride!

Suddenly, the giraffe gave a shout. He had seen something interesting.

"Hey!" he cried. "There's a whole tribe of monkeys hiding in the bushes!"

"Telinga cheated!" roared the animals. "His friends have helped him!"

The monkeys didn't wait to hear any more. They ran off, leaping into the trees to be out of reach.

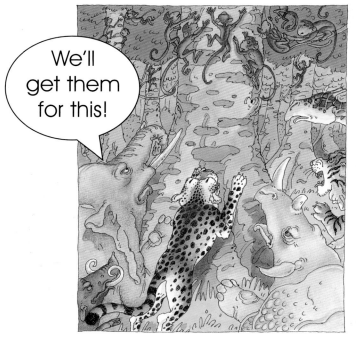

Monkeys have lived up in trees ever since. They're much too scared to come down.

## Chapter 3

# The rabbits and the crocodile

There was once a time when crocodiles lived on land, not in the water. One grumpy old crocodile lived near a river and lazed in the sun all day.

36

One day, a baby rabbit hopped past, looking for some tasty leaves.

"Hello!" he called and woke up the crocodile. The crocodile was furious.

Go away! I'm trying to sleep!

As the crocodile shut his eyes again, the rabbit hopped closer. He had spotted a bunch of fresh green leaves, just by the crocodile's nose.

With loud crunching, he began to gobble them up.

The crocodile's eyes snapped
open.

"Get away from those
leaves!" he roared. And he
snapped at the rabbit with
his enormous jaws.

The little rabbit ran and
ran. He didn't stop until he
reached his burrow.

"The crocodile nearly ate
me!" he told his mother. "But
I didn't do anything wrong."

I was only
eating some
leaves!

There,
there. You're
safe now!

His mother was very angry. "It's time that crocodile was taught a lesson," she said firmly. "He's grumpy and lazy and it just won't do."

Is everyone here?

Gathering the other rabbits together, she told them she had a plan.

41

The next day, the rabbits went into the woods. They collected branches, twigs and leaves and stuffed them into a sack.

Will... this... do..?

Almost full!

"That's enough!" said the rabbit's mother and off they went to find the crocodile.

They didn't have to look
far. He was by the riverbank,
asleep as usual. The rabbits
crept closer.

Zzzzzzzz...

Sneaking up, they made a
big circle of twigs, leaves and
branches around the crocodile.

Then the mother rabbit set light to the circle. The fire crackled and spat and smoke billowed up.

The crocodile woke with a jump. When he saw the fire, he bellowed in fear.

Help!
Fire!

The fire was licking at his  scales. Taking a flying leap, he jumped right over the flames...

...and disappeared into the river with a splash.

45

When the crocodile heard the rabbits laughing, he was very annoyed. He shouted at them from the river.

"Keep off our land then!" cried the rabbits and that's how it's stayed ever since.

Try these other books in
**Series One:**

**Dragons:** Stan must outwit a hungry dragon to feed his children. Victor must persuade two dragons not to eat him. Will they do it? Read these tales to find out.

**Magical Animals:** A horse that can fly? A creature that's half-lion, half-eagle? If you think they sound amazing, wait until you see the other animals in this book.

**The Dinosaurs Next Door:** Stan loves living next door to Mr. Puff. His house is full of amazing things. Best of all are the dinosaur eggs — until they begin to hatch...

**The Monster Gang:** Starting a gang is a great idea. So is dressing up like monsters. But if everyone is in disguise, how do you know who's who?

Series editor: Lesley Sims

Designed by
Katarina Dragoslavić

First published in 2007 by Usborne Publishing Ltd., Usborne House,
83-85 Saffron Hill, London EC1N 8RT, England. www.usborne.com
Copyright © 2007, 2003, 1989, 1982 Usborne Publishing Ltd.

48